LET SLEEPING DRAGONS LIE

Before Jimmy could talk him out of it, Chris crept closer to the dragon's nest. The creature was sound asleep, nestled in a mass of dead thorns and brambles. It was covered with green scales and bigger than three elephants. Every time it breathed out, flames shot from its nostrils.

Chris tiptoed around the beast, searching for the crystal. He spotted a stairway cut into the wall behind the dragon and started up it. At the top he discovered a glass case on a marble pedestal. Inside it was a single large crystal, surrounded by six slight depressions, on a red velvet cushion.

It was bigger and more beautiful than Chris had even dreamed. He took it out of the case and held it gently in his hand. The crystal sparkled with every color of the rainbow.

"Hurry, Chris. It's awake!"

GARY PAULSEN

WORLD OF ADVENTURE

THE SEVENTH
CRYSTAL

A YEARLING BOOK

Published by
Bantam Doubleday Dell Books for Young Readers
a division of
Bantam Doubleday Dell Publishing Group, Inc.
1540 Broadway
New York, New York 10036

ISBN: 0-440-41051-7

Series design: Barbara Berger

Interior illustration by Michael David Biegel

Printed in the United States of America

August 1996

OPM   10   9   8   7   6   5   4   3   2   1

Dear Readers:

Real adventure is many things—it's danger and daring and sometimes even a struggle for life or death. From competing in the Iditarod dogsled race across Alaska to sailing the Pacific Ocean, I've experienced some of this adventure myself. I try to capture this spirit in my stories, and each time I sit down to write, that challenge is a bit of an adventure in itself.

You're all a part of this adventure as well. Over the years I've had the privilege of talking with many of you in schools, and this book is the result of hearing firsthand what you want to read about most—power-packed action and excitement.

You asked for it—so hang on tight while we jump into another thrilling story in my World of Adventure.

Gary Paulsen

THE SEVENTH CRYSTAL

CHAPTER 1

Chris Masters watched the clock on the classroom wall. His palms had begun sweating. There was nothing on his desk. He'd already stuffed his books and papers into his backpack.

Timing was crucial. He tried not to blink, so that he wouldn't miss the exact instant the minute hand began to move.

The long black hand of the clock edged forward. His heart started beating faster. He turned sideways in his desk and sat in a crouched position, his left foot slightly behind his right.

Ten more seconds.

A deep voice thundered from the front of the room. "Mr. Masters, can you repeat the instructions I just gave the class?"

Chris's whole body tensed. The bell rang, but Mr. Higgins, the science teacher, ordered the students to remain in their seats. Cynthia Rider, Lincoln Junior High's head cheerleader, glared at Chris for holding up the class.

Mr. Higgins walked slowly down the aisle, holding a wooden ruler. He stopped in front of Chris's desk and pointed the ruler at him. "Well?"

Chris ran his hand through his short brown hair, lowered his eyes, and tried to think. He had been so intent on the clock that he hadn't heard a word Mr. Higgins had said in the past five minutes. He made a feeble stab at an answer. "Did you tell us to have a nice weekend?"

The class roared with laughter. Mr. Higgins's face turned red clear up to his bald spot.

"No. I did not." The teacher took a deep

breath and tried to regain his composure. "The rest of the class is dismissed. Mr. Masters, you will stay and write *In the future, I will pay attention in class* five hundred times."

"But Mr. Higgins, you don't understand. If I don't . . . I mean if they get ahead of me . . ."

"Yes?"

Chris slumped miserably in his desk and sighed. "Nothing." He was dead meat. There was no way he could explain to Mr. Higgins that every day at three o'clock he ran a race to save his life. Well, maybe not his life, at least not yet. But it was definitely a race for his physical well-being. That and any money he might have saved from lunch.

Shawn Stiles was the oldest and biggest kid at Lincoln. He and his friend Cliff Bacon made a career out of pushing the other students around. Lately they had targeted Chris, and for the past two weeks they had been waiting for him after school. When they caught him, they slapped him around and took anything he had that they wanted.

Chris knew better than to rat on the two bullies. If he did they would never let up on him.
So he handled it by being the first and fastest
kid to leave the school grounds every day.

Except today.

CHAPTER 2

 Chris walked out the double doors beside Mr. Higgins. The teacher had lectured him all the way down the hall about the importance of staying alert. Occasionally Chris nodded to make it seem as if he were paying attention.

Actually Chris *was* alert. He'd already checked out the parking lot and watched for movement behind the Dumpster. The shadows at the end of the building worried him. But then so did the trees by the fence.

Mr. Higgins stepped into his old blue sedan and rolled the window down. "You're a good student, Chris, but you'd be doing us both a favor if you'd pay more attention."

"Right. Thanks, Mr. Higgins." Chris waved and darted behind the next car, crouched low, and scuttled through the remaining row of parked cars.

At the last car he stopped and scanned the area. No one was in sight. So far so good. He could see the sidewalk where Shawn and Cliff, grinning and howling like hungry hyenas, usually waited. They weren't there.

It looked clear to the oak tree. Chris's hopes soared. Maybe they'd gotten tired of waiting and had crawled back into their holes.

Cautiously he rose from his hiding place and moved to the fence. If he could make it past the oak tree, he could blast across the street and run all the way home.

His feet flew. Everything around him was a blur. He made it to the fence. Quickly he shoved his backpack through a jagged hole and started to climb through after it.

"What's the big hurry, Chris?"

Chris had one leg through the hole in the

fence. He looked up. Shawn had stepped from behind the oak tree and was standing over him, smirking. Chris pulled his leg back and turned to run.

"Now, don't do that." Cliff had already swung around the fence and cut off Chris's escape. "We have some business to take care of, remember?"

Chris took a step backward. Cliff grabbed the front of his T-shirt and pushed him into the fence. "You better have something good for us after keeping us waiting all this time, shrimp."

"Look, guys," Chris said, gulping, "I'm not carrying anything you'd want. My grandmother forgot to give me my lunch money. All I had for lunch was an apple left over from yesterday."

Shawn picked up Chris's backpack and rummaged through it. "You know, Chris, it looks like you may be telling the truth this time." The hulking boy turned the pack upside down and dumped Chris's books and papers on the sidewalk. "But since we know how much you hate to disappoint us, we'll just take this fine backpack your granny bought you."

Cliff laughed. He twisted the collar of Chris's shirt even tighter. "Thanks, Chris."

"What's going on here?"

Chris felt Cliff release his grip. The bigger boy stepped back and put his hands innocently into his pockets.

Chris wheeled around. He couldn't believe his luck. Mr. Higgins had driven up beside them.

Shawn knelt and started putting books back into Chris's bag. "There's nothing going on, Mr. Higgins. Chris here just dropped his backpack, and Cliff and I were being neighborly. You know, helping him pick up his stuff."

Mr. Higgins's eyes narrowed suspiciously. "Is that right, Chris?"

Chris nervously scratched the back of his neck. "That—That's right. They were helping me."

Shawn handed him the backpack. "Here you go, Chris." He slapped Chris hard on the back. "We like helping out our good friend Chris. Don't we, Cliff?"

Cliff nodded, and the two bullies sauntered down the sidewalk. Shawn looked back over his shoulder. "Don't worry, Chris, we'll always be around to *help* you."

Chris breathed a sigh of relief as he watched them leave. He picked up the rest of his papers and had started to cram them into his pack when he noticed that Mr. Higgins was still there watching him, waiting for an explanation.

Chris gave the teacher a halfhearted smile, backed down the sidewalk a few feet, shrugged—and ran.

Chapter 3

"I'm home, Grandma." Chris dropped his backpack onto one of the kitchen chairs and took the lid off the cookie jar. It was full of freshly made chocolate chip cookies. He put one in his mouth and scooped up a handful to take to his room.

From the living room he could hear the television blaring. His grandmother was watching her favorite soap opera. He decided not to bother her and instead went straight upstairs to get down to business.

Business consisted of trying to find the secret path to the ancient palace in the Valley of

Zon. He'd been working on this particular computer game for almost three days and had made it only as far as the River of Storms.

It was unusual for Chris to have trouble with any video or computer game. Most of them were too easy for him. His mind just seemed to know what was going to happen before the computer made it occur.

But this game was special. It had come in the mail three days ago with no return address and very few instructions. The first night he worked on it until two in the morning. The graphics looked so three-dimensional that when he turned it on, it almost seemed as if the people and places were real.

The game opened with a medieval scene—a huge castle shrouded in fog. Then words scrolled up the screen, telling the mysterious legend of a beautiful princess with magical powers. This princess ruled her people well until a disloyal knight kidnapped her. Using black magic, he turned her into a statue so that he could steal her kingdom.

The object of the game was to make it through all the traps and hazards the black knight had laid for those who might follow him, and then discover a way to free the princess.

The first time Chris played the game he was chased by creatures that spit fire. Then he'd gone in circles for hours until he'd stumbled on a magic compass, which led him to the river.

The next day he had found a hidden cave in a forest. But the cave didn't lead anywhere and there didn't seem to be a way out of it.

Chris sat down at his desk and switched on his computer. He took a deep breath. "No game is gonna get the best of me."

The title screen lit up in an array of dazzling color. The words *The Seventh Crystal* appeared in bold print, followed by the picture of the castle. Chris pushed the Start button. A young boy wearing a ragged brown peasant's costume ran down a dusty path. The boy passed several village people coming and going near a grassy meadow. Suddenly two thieves jumped in front of him and tried to block his path. Chris pushed the Jump button and sailed over the attackers. They were chasing the boy, and he had no weapon for protection.

Chris paused the game. He knew how to get to the forest, but he didn't want to get stuck in the cave again. He closed his eyes and tried to imagine what he would do next if he had created this game.

Suddenly his bedroom door flew open with a bang. "Hey. Are you getting anywhere with that?"

Chris spun his chair around. Standing in front of him was a stocky redheaded boy whose face was covered with freckles.

"I just got started, Jimmy. I'll beat it, though. You know they haven't made the game that can stop me."

Jimmy Johnson was Chris's next-door neighbor and best friend. Jimmy was a year younger than Chris and still went to Taft Middle School.

"You were late coming home, Chris. Did they get you today?"

"Yeah. But it worked out all right. A teacher

drove up just in time." Chris turned back to the game. "You want to watch?"

"Maybe for a while. My mom says I have to be home early. My dad is coming to get me for the weekend."

"Where's he taking you this time?"

Jimmy sat on the edge of the bed. "Who knows? Did you get out of the cave yet?"

Chris shook his head. "I started over. I figured I must have missed something along the way that would let me out of it." He studied the computer screen. "I don't see anything. Do you?"

"Why don't you ask some of those people on the path?"

Chris looked up and smiled. "Jimmy, you're a genius." He started the game again and used his mouse to maneuver the peasant boy so that he made contact with the images of the villagers on the path. Nothing happened until he came across the image of an old woman.

She was waiting in the meadow, not scurrying around like the rest of the people, just sitting patiently under a tree. When the peasant boy stopped in front of her, she gave him a toothless grin and put something round in his hand.

"What is it?" Jimmy asked. He moved closer to the screen.

"I can't tell for sure. But I hope it helps me get out of the cave."

"What's she saying?"

Words appeared in a green box at the top of the screen. Chris read them aloud. " 'The lion's mouth at the Palace of Zon is the only way to save the princess.' "

Jimmy looked puzzled. "What's Zon?"

Chris paused the game and took an envelope out of his desk drawer. He opened it and showed Jimmy the letter inside. "This came with the game."

Chosen One,

The ancient palace lies in the Valley of Zon. It is imperative that you come immediately. You are my last hope. Look for the secret path. The stars will lead the way. Take care. The eyes of Mogg are everywhere.

Darvina

Jimmy moved back. "Those are weird instructions. Have you figured out who sent the game to you?"

"Nope. But I'm glad they did. It's been a long time since I've played anything that was this much of a challenge."

"Jimmy, are you up there?" Chris's grandmother shouted from the bottom of the stairs.

Chris went to the landing. "He's here, Grandma."

"Tell him his mother wants him to run down to the store for her before his father comes to get him."

Chris turned and was about to repeat the message. Jimmy held his hand up. "I heard. Want to come with me? I hate crossing over those old subway tunnels. They give me the creeps."

Chris glanced at the game. He hated to waste precious time that could be used to defeat it. Then he looked at Jimmy. It was obvious that his friend wanted him to go. The shortcut over the tunnels saved time, but it was dangerous. The city had put up No Trespassing signs and an old chain-link fence blocking the tunnels off from the general public, but everyone still cut across them.

Chris walked to the computer, saved his game, and turned it off. "Sure, I'll go with you. I can work on this old thing anytime."

CHAPTER 4

"Don't forget to get skim milk, Jimmy. The cheap brand." Jimmy's mother looked at Chris and raised an eyebrow. "And don't waste any time at the arcade."

"Okay, okay." Jimmy took the money she handed him and waved for Chris to follow him out the front door.

"She treats me like a baby," Jimmy complained when they were outside the fence around the yard.

"Don't worry." Chris kicked a rock down

the sidewalk. "They seem to grow out of it when you get to junior high."

"Can't be too soon for me." Jimmy stuffed the money in his front pocket. "Want to cut through the park?"

"Why not? Race you to the fountain."

Chris gave Jimmy a small head start and then sprinted after him. They made it to the fountain at the same time. Jimmy was breathing hard and sat down on the concrete edge.

Chris looked up at the statue in the middle of the old fountain. It was a girl holding her hands out. No water flowed out of the fountain now. It was covered with rust, and a bluish green slime had started to form where the water used to be.

He had never really looked at the girl before, but for some reason today he couldn't take his eyes off her face. She looked so sad, almost as if she would cry if she could manage it.

"Come on." Jimmy pushed him gently. "We better get to the store or I'm gonna be in trouble."

Chris backed away from the statue and reluctantly turned to follow his friend. He shook his head. What was the matter with him today? Three steps later, he tripped on something in the grass and almost fell.

"Are you okay?" Jimmy asked, picking up a dirt-covered metallic gadget from the grass. He started to throw it back down, but changed his mind and slid it into his jacket pocket.

"Yeah, I'm fine." Chris scrambled to his feet. "I don't know what's wrong with—" He stopped. Directly in front of them was an elderly woman sitting under a tree. Chris blinked. It couldn't be. She looked exactly like the woman in the video game.

The woman beckoned him with her long, gnarled fingers. Chris didn't move. Then she gave him a toothless smile.

"It's her!" Chris whispered.

"What are you talking about?" Jimmy pulled on Chris's sleeve. "Let's go."

"In a minute." Chris shrugged him off and moved closer to the woman. She was holding something out to him. He hesitated, then stepped up and took it. The small object was round and black with age.

"Uh . . . thanks," he said, stepping back. The old woman just nodded and smiled serenely.

"What did she give you?" Jimmy whispered.

Chris handed it to his friend. "I don't know. It sort of looks like an old subway token."

Chris turned back to ask the woman why she had given it to him.

She was gone. His eyes scanned the park. She had disappeared.

Jimmy gave the token back to him. "Come on, Chris. I'm gonna be busted if I'm late."

Chris closed his hand around the token. He walked along beside Jimmy in silence, thinking. What a weird coincidence, if it was a coincidence. The odds of something like this happening were pretty small, impossible in fact.

They were walking over the old tunnels and Jimmy was mumbling something about the city needing to fill them up before somebody got hurt again. He and Chris used to play in them when they were younger, until Jimmy fell through some boards and the fire department had to come get him out.

Chris's mind wasn't on the tunnels. He was thinking about the old woman. If he had been paying attention he would have heard the fast footsteps closing in behind them.

"Well, well. If it isn't Chris and his little dork friend." Shawn folded his arms and talked while Cliff circled in front of them. "What are you girls doing way out here?"

Chris clenched his fist. "You go on to the store, Jimmy. I'll be there in a minute."

"Look, hero." Cliff grabbed Chris's arm and twisted it. "The dork can go when we say he can."

"Did you hear that, Cliff?" Shawn sneered. "Little Jimmy is on the way to the store. How much money do you think his mommy gave him?"

Chris tried to squirm out of Cliff's grip, but it was too tight.

Jimmy was small, but he wasn't a coward. He bent over and charged at Cliff like a bull.

Shawn stuck out his leg and tripped the

younger boy. Jimmy slid facefirst into the black dirt.

"Cut it out, Shawn." Chris's dark eyes flashed. "We'll give you the money. Just leave him alone."

"Now, that's more like it." Shawn smiled coldly. "Where is it?"

"It's in my shoe. Tell this big ape to let go of me and I'll get it for you."

Shawn nodded at Cliff and he let go of Chris's arm. Chris reached down as if he were going to untie his shoe. Instead he scooped up a handful of dirt and threw it in Shawn's face.

"Run, Jimmy!"

Shawn wiped at his eyes and snarled, "Get them!"

Chris darted down some concrete steps that used to lead to the subway and jumped over a chain into the closest tunnel entrance, with Jimmy right on his heels. It was dark, and the farther they ran the darker it became, but they kept running.

Behind them they heard the two bullies yelling. "Which way did they go, Cliff? I'm gonna kill that kid this time."

"They're getting closer," Jimmy wailed between breaths.

"Keep running." Chris charged through the blackness without a clue where he was headed. Then—*wham!* It felt as if he had hit a wall.

The feeling lasted only a second. A brilliant white light flooded the tunnel. Chris knew his feet were still moving—but it felt as if he were floating.

And then he lost consciousness.

CHAPTER 5

Chris sat up and slowly opened his eyes. The sky was a brilliant blue, and the trees and bushes around him looked greener than any he had ever seen. He felt strange, out of place. His mind whirled. Where was he? The last thing he could remember was the white light.

He heard a low groan and looked behind him. Jimmy was stretched out near a solid rock wall. Shawn Stiles was on the ground beside him. They were both just waking up.

Jimmy propped himself up on his elbows

25

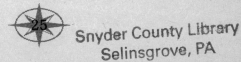

and squinted at Chris. "Why are you dressed like that?"

Chris looked down at himself. He was wearing a ragged brown sacklike shirt that barely came to his knees, with a rope for a belt, and brown shoes with pointed toes. "I . . . I don't know." He fingered the odd cloth in amazement.

Shawn moaned and held his head. "Did a train hit us? Are we dead?" He looked at Chris and snickered. "Who are you supposed to be? Peter Pan?"

"I've got a real bad feeling about this, Chris." Jimmy was on his feet now, looking at the countryside. "Where have we seen cone-shaped trees like this before?"

Chris's eyes were wide and his voice was shaky. "In the video game."

"What are you two nerds talking about?" Shawn gazed around. "Where are we?"

Chris ignored him. "It was the token, Jimmy. Remember, in the game at home I was looking for a way out of the cave and the old woman under the tree gave me something to help me?"

Jimmy nodded. "That woman in the park gave you the token and we blasted through the end of the subway tunnel—right into the game. You're the boy in The Seventh Crystal."

Shawn staggered to his feet. "If one of you dweebs don't tell me what's going on real soon I'm gonna—"

"You're gonna what?" Chris asked. "Your pet gorilla, Cliff, isn't here to do your dirty work for you. He's probably still in the tunnel trying to figure out where you went. Come on Jimmy, let's go. There's got to be a way out of this place."

Jimmy took a step and paused. "Chris, this is scary. We might have a better chance of getting out of here if we all worked together."

Chris rolled his eyes. "We're in some deep stuff here, Jimmy. The last thing we need is dead weight."

"Who are you calling—" Shawn stopped because of the noise. The others heard it too. It was a loud buzzing sound.

From out of nowhere a ball of fire hit the ground near Chris's feet. He leaped to the side and glanced up. The sky was filled with scorpionlike creatures spitting flames. Fireballs were landing all around them.

"Run for it!" Chris yelled. He dodged some sparks, bolted for the cover of the woods, and dived into the underbrush.

The scorpion creatures chased them as far as the first row of trees and stopped. They hovered for a few seconds, dropped several more fireballs, then flew away.

When the buzzing noise had died, Chris raised his head and whispered, "Jimmy? Are you all right?"

The brush beside him rustled, and Jimmy crawled out. "I'm okay. But boy, that was close."

Shawn crawled toward them. "What were those things?"

Chris stepped out of the brush and sat down next to Jimmy. He studied Shawn. "I probably shouldn't tell you anything, but Jimmy might have a point. We may need you."

"For what? Where are we?"

"This is going to sound crazy, but somehow we've been transported to the inside of a computer game. I know it's hard to believe. I'm not really sure I believe it myself."

Shawn gave a hollow laugh. "That's a good one." He stood up. "Okay, I give. You nerds win. Cliff and I won't bother you anymore, just tell me what's really going on. I've got stuff to do."

Chris continued. "It's called The Seventh Crystal. Someone sent the game to my house a couple of days ago. I don't know much about it. I barely got started on it. All I know is, if we want to get home, we have to find the way out."

Shawn raised his eyebrows at Jimmy. "He's kidding, right?"

Jimmy shook his head.

"Well, I'm not falling for your stupid joke." Shawn headed for the path. "I'm going home right now."

When he stepped out of the woods the buzzing sound started again.

"Get back here, stupid!" Chris shouted. "Those fireballs are real."

Shawn swallowed. He stayed at the edge of

the woods until he saw the first flying scorpion. Then he ran for cover.

Once again the scorpions hovered near the first row of trees and then, after a few seconds, flew away.

When the noise stopped, Shawn crawled to the spot where Jimmy and Chris were waiting. "Okay. I'll go along with this stupid theory for now. But the first chance I get to leave, I'm outta here."

Chapter 6

"Okay, let's think about this logically." Chris was talking more to himself than to anyone else. He pushed some branches aside. "If this is a game, then everything that happens is already planned. The flamethrowers can't get any closer than the first row of trees, so if we stay to the side of the path we'll be fine."

Shawn elbowed Jimmy. "Does he always talk to himself?"

"Sometimes. Chris is a computer game wizard. If anybody can get us out of this, he can."

Chris made his way through the trees, trying to keep the path in sight and still stay far enough away from the flying scorpions. They walked for what seemed like hours, until Jimmy noticed something.

"Uh, Chris. I don't know for sure, but isn't that the same rock wall we started from?" Jimmy pointed through the trees.

Chris sighed. "I was afraid of that. We've been going around in circles. It happened in the game at home until I stumbled on a magic compass. Looks like we're going nowhere without it."

Shawn turned on Jimmy. "I thought you said he was a genius or something. He can't even get us away from where we started."

Jimmy frowned and put his hands in his pockets. When he did, his fingers touched the thing Chris had tripped over in the park. His face lit up. "Did you say you *stumbled* on the compass?"

"Yeah." Chris nodded. "The kid in the game sort of tripped on it."

Jimmy handed the strange object to Chris. "Did it look like this?"

Chris's mouth fell open. "Where did you . . ."

"In the park." Jimmy smiled. "Remember, you tripped on something right before you saw the old woman?"

"All right!" Chris took the oddly shaped silver compass and wiped the dirt off it. A long metal arrow moved grudgingly, then stopped. Chris held the compass out and began walking in the direction the arrow pointed. "Now we're getting somewhere."

The compass took them up a steep hill and across the path twice. Flamethrowers appeared both times, but the boys were too fast for them.

From the top of the hill they could see a beautiful green valley below. And nestled at the far northern end was a small village.

As they neared the little town, Chris noticed that the people there didn't seem to be troubled by the scorpions. They were walking around normally, as if the scorpions didn't exist. He decided to see if the scorpions were still a problem and stepped out of the trees and onto the path.

Nothing happened. Chris motioned for the other two boys to come out of hiding. "We must finally be out of the flamethrowers' territory."

"Good." Shawn brushed a leaf and a few twigs out of his hair. "Maybe we can go into that dumpy town and make a couple of phone calls. Somebody's bound to be able to come pick us up."

Jimmy tapped Chris on the back. "Somehow I don't think he gets it yet."

"Listen, Shawn, you'd better let me do the talking down there," Chris said. "We don't know if this town is friendly or not."

"Who cares?" Shawn sneered at him. "I told you, Chris, the first chance I get, I'm outta here." He strode down the path. "I'm leaving. You geeks are on your own."

CHAPTER 7

Shawn trotted down the hill ahead of Chris and Jimmy. They watched as he stopped near a wooden cart full of various types of fruit and spoke to an elderly man who tended it. "Hey, old-timer. Where's the phone in this town?"

The man stared at him, wiped his hands on his long leather apron, and without a word pushed his cart down the road.

"I told you to let me do the talking," Chris said smugly as they caught up with Shawn. "These people wouldn't trust you. Look at the way you're dressed."

"What's wrong with the way I'm dressed?" Shawn inspected his clothes. His T-shirt had a skull and crossbones on the front with the name of a heavy-metal rock group across the bottom.

"The people here might be superstitious. So just let me handle it."

Chris spotted a young woman with long golden-blond hair who was about to go inside one of the thatch-roofed wooden houses. He hurried up the street. "Excuse me, miss. Could I talk to you a minute?"

The girl shifted the basket she was holding to her other arm and waited for him to continue.

"I, that is we, are in sort of a weird situation here and we were wondering if you might be able to help us."

"Yes?"

"We're looking for information about the Seventh Crystal."

The girl gasped, rushed inside the small cottage, and slammed the door.

"Real smooth, Chris," Shawn laughed.

"You definitely know how to get through to these people."

Thundering hoofbeats suddenly echoed in the distance. Soon several riders on large black horses emerged, charging through the village, scattering people as they went. A woman screamed, and people started running. Mothers scooped up their small children and hurried indoors.

"Quickly," a voice behind them whispered. "Come inside before it's too late." The golden-haired girl who had been carrying the basket had opened the thick wooden door of her cottage and was standing in the shadows, urging them to come in.

The three boys ducked inside the dark cottage, and she shut the door behind them. From the window they could see the village square. Five massive horses were pawing the ground, steam bursting from their nostrils.

The riders of the beasts were at least twice the size of normal men. They wore shiny black armor with headpieces resembling dragons and other hideous monsters.

Two of the knights quickly climbed down from their mounts and dragged the old man who had been selling fruit into the middle of the street. They threw him to the ground in front of the horse of the largest knight.

The one who appeared to be the leader stepped off his horse and bellowed, "Tell us if you've seen the warrior!"

The old man was shaking so hard that he couldn't speak. He kissed the boots of the leader as if begging for mercy. In a flash the giant knight drew a strange, glowing green sword and lopped off the fruit seller's head.

The severed head flew up in the air, spewing blood as it went. When it finally landed, the leader kicked it down the dusty street like a child kicking a ball.

Then he turned, held his sword out, and roared. "Let this be a lesson to all of you. Mogg demands loyalty. If the warrior comes to this town, turn him away—or die."

Chapter 8

"It is well that you have seen the vile acts of the knights of Mogg."

Chris jumped at the sound of the raspy voice. An old man with a long, flowing white beard was sitting in the shadows at a carved wooden table. He wore a blue robe over his tunic and held a tall staff in his right hand.

The man rose and hobbled across the sparsely furnished room to a rug near the hearth. He flicked it aside with his staff, revealing a trapdoor. He fixed his ancient eyes on Chris. "Come, warrior."

Chris looked at the girl. "Does he mean me?"

She nodded. "My grandfather, Wizard of Gothan and Keeper of the Stars, believes you are the chosen one. I told him you inquired about the Seventh Crystal."

The old man stroked his long beard and thoughtfully studied Jimmy and Shawn. "Are your servants trustworthy, warrior?"

"Servants?" Shawn made a face and started to explain.

Chris cut him off. "My servants can be trusted. Will you show us the way to the Seventh Crystal?"

"Granddaughter," the wizard ordered, "the warrior's servants will stay with you for a time. Give them food, and be careful to let no one see them. The eyes of Mogg are in this town."

He lifted the trapdoor and disappeared down the stone steps.

Jimmy looked worried. "How do you know you can trust this guy, Chris?"

"I don't. But the way I see it, we're a little short of choices right now." Chris stepped down into the opening. The girl shut the trapdoor and covered it with the rug.

At first Chris couldn't see a thing. He had to feel his way down the steps. At the bottom, the narrow opening became larger, and along the rock walls in front of him hung several lit torches.

Chris saw the hem of the blue robe turn right a few yards ahead of him. He moved faster, trying to catch up. The rock walls gave way to dirt, and the passage smelled musty and damp. He made another right turn and stopped.

The old man was waiting for him in a small candlelit room. There were tables on which containers stood, filled with colored liquids that dripped through coils into smaller containers. It reminded Chris of Mr. Higgins's science lab back at school.

A strange book lay open on a pedestal in the center of the room. Chris went to it but couldn't read any of the words. It was written in a language he had never seen.

"So you've come looking for the Seventh Crystal?" The old wizard sat on a stool near a battered chest. "What abilities do you possess? Do you fight well? Are you a magician?"

Chris scratched his head. "I'm not sure I have any abilities."

"Ahhh, humility. This is good." The wizard opened the lid of the tattered chest and lifted something out.

"This is for you, warrior." He handed Chris a long glowing green sword like the one the black knight had used to behead the fruit seller. "It is ten times greater than that of the knights of Mogg. It is the only weapon that will defeat the dragon."

"Dragon?" Chris took the sword. "I didn't know there was a dragon in this game." He swung it over his head, fighting a make-believe enemy. "Thanks."

"Do not thank me. It is yours by destiny." The old man turned to a smaller chest, took a brass key from the folds of his robe, and unlocked the chest. "My next gift is very special. You will require it to complete your appointed task."

When the chest was opened, Chris saw a long gold chain with three gold stars hanging from it. The wizard took it from the chest and slipped it over Chris's head. "These are the magic stars of the Princess Darvina. They have great power, so be careful that they do not fall into the wrong hands."

Chris slid the sword into his rope belt. "Would you mind answering a few questions for me?"

The old wizard's eyes sparkled. "You are not like the others. They would not ask questions. They were foolish."

"Others?"

"There were six before you, all brave knights of the highest caliber. They too went on the quest to save Darvina. But, alas, they failed and were turned into statues for eternity. They accomplished nothing except to use up six of the seven crystals that might have saved our beloved princess. It is now left to you alone. There is only one crystal remaining in the dragon's lair. The Princess Darvina has sent for you, warrior. You are her last hope."

"How do I get this crystal?"

"The crystal is in the dragon's lair, past the

River of Storms and the Death Swamp. The way is difficult, but remember that a wise man's heart is at his right hand and a fool's heart is at his left."

"What do I do with the crystal after I get it?"

"*If* you are able to obtain the crystal, travel to the palace in Zon where the princess is held captive. Mogg has placed a powerful spell on the palace which only a crystal can unlock."

The old man put his wrinkled hand on Chris's shoulder. "Guard the crystal well, my son. If Mogg or his evil knights get their hands on it, our world will be lost."

CHAPTER 9

"Did the wizard tell you what the stars are for?" Jimmy asked.

"Right before we left his house, he said that when the time was right I would know." Chris threw a rock in the river. "He also said they belonged to the princess and if we find her we're supposed to give them back."

"Who cares about a dumb old princess? I thought you were gonna find out how to get us out of this stupid game." Shawn scratched his cheek and looked down at the water. "I'm sick of this whole thing."

"Nobody asked you to come," Chris

snapped. "In fact, none of us would be here if you and Cliff hadn't been chasing us." He turned to Jimmy. "The wizard said we have to cross the River of Storms and go on to the Death Swamp. The crystal is on an island guarded by a man-eating dragon."

"That figures." Jimmy stared at the river in front of them. "Any ideas how we're going to get across this?"

Shawn stepped off the bank and waded out into the clear blue water. "It doesn't look that far. We can swim across."

"I wouldn't do that if I were you." Chris folded his arms.

"Give it a rest, Mr. Know-it-all. I'm getting out of here!" With that, Shawn plunged farther into the river.

Chris glanced up. "They don't call it the River of Storms for nothing." A dark cloud had formed over Shawn's head. The wind started to blow, and giant drops of rain began to fall. Lightning flashed, and the rain turned to hail.

Shawn fought his way back to shore through the pelting ice. He stood on the bank shivering, watching the clouds disappear. "Why didn't someone tell me?"

Jimmy shrugged. "You didn't ask."

Chris took out the compass. The arrow spun three times before settling on a direction upstream. "Let's see where this thing leads us."

They left the path and traveled up the bank about thirty yards, where they came to an old boat dock. The compass changed directions and pointed across the river.

"This must be the spot." Chris tucked the compass inside his shirt and scanned the area for some kind of raft.

"You're on a roll, Chris." Shawn inspected the area under the dock. "How are you gonna get across with no boat?"

"In most of the games I've played before like this, one just appears for you—if you hit the right spot on the game field." Chris stepped to the edge of the dock. "I guess this one's different." He put one foot out above the water. The dark cloud immediately formed above them.

"Wait, Chris. What are you doing?" Jimmy moved up beside his friend.

"Trust me. I've seen it work this way before." Chris closed his eyes and stepped off the dock.

He didn't fall into the water. Instead he found himself standing on an invisible bridge. He pulled out the compass. It pointed straight ahead. A violent storm raged on both sides, but the path in front of him was clear all the way across.

Jimmy stepped down behind him. "You did it." He looked back at Shawn. "I told you he was a genius."

CHAPTER 10

"I can hardly see my hand in front of my face," Shawn complained. "Are you sure you're going the right way?"

A thick fog had surrounded them when they started through the swamp. Mud sucked at their shoes and made walking difficult. Chris had to hold the compass close to see the arrow. "We should keep going this way."

At a fork in the trail, the fog lifted slightly. One path was dry and clear; the other looked as if it was deep swampy mud all the way. Chris held up the compass, turning it one way and then another. "It's pointing at the right fork."

"Well, you're crazy if you think I'm going that way." Shawn started down the left trail. "See you at the island."

Jimmy made a face and stepped into the knee-deep mud behind Chris. "Are you sure we have to go this way? Maybe there's more than one trail that leads to the island."

"Most games have something like this in them to throw you off the track. It'll get better, don't worry."

"Do you think we should have let Shawn go off on his own like that?"

"What is it with you, Jimmy? That jerk tried to steal your money earlier and now you're worried about him?"

"It's just that this game is so real. Shawn doesn't seem to know that it could kill him."

The words of the wizard flashed through Chris's mind. "A wise man's heart is at his right hand and a fool's heart is at his left." He stopped. "We'd better go back for him. I think the wizard tried to warn me about that left trail."

A piercing scream ripped through the misty air.

"It's Shawn!" Chris moved as fast as he could through the thick mud. When he reached the dry path he started running.

Shawn was nowhere in sight. Chris retraced his steps.

"Help me!"

"There he is." Jimmy pointed off to the side of the path. In a pond of bubbling black ooze they saw Shawn's head and shoulders. A long, shiny red tentacle was wrapped around his body and was slowly pulling him deeper into the bog.

Chris drew his sword and jumped in. A tentacle snaked out and grabbed at his foot. He slashed at it and kept moving.

All he could see of Shawn now was the top of his head. The creature had pulled him almost completely under. Chris hacked at the curled tentacle. A warm, stinking green slime squirted out and landed on Chris's face and clothes. He kept hacking until he could get a grip on one of Shawn's arms.

When Jimmy saw what Chris was trying to

do, he waded through the bog and helped pull on Shawn's free arm. A tentacle started for Jimmy, but Chris saw it coming and sliced the end off. The creature recoiled, let go of Shawn, and slithered away.

Chris took one arm, and Jimmy took the other. Shawn hung between them like a limp noodle as they dragged him back to the path.

Jimmy watched Chris roll Shawn over and push on his stomach, trying to get the boy to breathe. "Is . . . he gonna live?"

Shawn coughed and spit out a mouthful of mud and brown water. "Of course I'm gonna live, geekwad. What took you guys so long, anyway? I could have died out there."

Chris sat back on his heels and looked up at Jimmy. "I say we throw him back in."

CHAPTER 11

"Are you sure you lost it?"

"I'm sure, Jimmy. I had it in my shirt right before I went in after Shawn."

"What's the big deal about a stupid compass, anyway?" Shawn pointed to the island in front of them. "We're here, aren't we? Let's just get the crystal and get out of here."

"You want me to go back and look for it?" Jimmy offered.

Chris shook his head. "It's probably at the bottom of the swamp with whatever that thing was by now. I guess from here on we'll just have to rely on instinct." He led the way across a stone bridge onto the rocky island. There were paths going in every direction. This time he chose the one to the right without any complaints from Shawn.

The trail took them up a rugged, tree-clad mountainside and stopped at the face of a glistening, sheer rock wall.

"What now, Boy Scout? You gonna fly over it?" Shawn reached out to lean against the wall. The rock disappeared, and he fell through.

"It's an illusion!" Chris shouted. He cautiously stepped through the rock wall into a large cavern.

"What happened?" Shawn sat up and rubbed his elbow.

"A miracle—you finally did something useful." Chris waited for Jimmy to come through the wall. "This must be the dragon's lair." He took out his sword. "You and Shawn don't have to come. This next part could be dangerous."

"Sounds good to me." Shawn made himself

comfortable on the ground. "Call us when you get the crystal."

"We'd better go with you," Jimmy said. "You might need our help."

"What is this *we* business?" Shawn asked. "If the hero wants to go alone, let him."

"We started this together, and we'll finish it together." Jimmy folded his arms tightly across his chest.

"Geeeezz." Shawn stood up. "You'd think we were the Three Musketeers or something."

Chris smiled in spite of himself. He couldn't imagine three more unlikely musketeers. "All right then, come on. I have no idea what's waiting for us."

They stayed close to the wall of the cavern and cautiously made their way to the back. Near the back a horrid odor filled the stale air, and they saw a strange orange light that would flare and then disappear.

"Ugh." Shawn held his nose. "Somebody needs to empty the litter box."

"What's that light?" Jimmy whispered.

"Dragon breath." Chris knelt behind a boulder. He could see the dragon's tail. It was long with a spike at the end. His heart started to race. He spoke in a low voice. "I doubt if it's just going to let us stroll in there and take the crystal. We need a plan."

"Plan? We need an army." Shawn's eyes narrowed. "Didn't that wizard tell you how to keep from turning into a shish kebab?"

"Not really. He just said to use the sword. I was hoping we might be able to sneak up on the dragon while it was asleep."

"Be my guest, Chris. I'd have to be invisible before I'd try a stunt like that."

Chris sighed. "Right now I wish I was invisible."

"Chris! Where'd you go?" Jimmy reached for the spot where Chris had been. He could feel a shoulder and face.

"Stop that." Chris pushed Jimmy's hand away. "What are you doing?"

"I—I can't see you. You disappeared."

"Really?" Chris touched the chain he wore around his neck, whistling in disbelief. "It has to be these magic stars. The old wizard said they would come in handy."

"You want me to do it too?" Jimmy reached for the necklace.

"Not this time. You guys wait here. I'll be back in a flash with the crystal."

Before Jimmy could talk him out of it, Chris crept closer to the dragon's nest. The creature was sound asleep, nestled in a mass of dead thorns and brambles. It was covered with green scales and bigger than three elephants. Every time it breathed out, flames shot from its nostrils.

Chris tiptoed around the beast, searching for the crystal. He spotted a stairway cut into the wall behind the dragon and started up it. At the top he discovered a glass case on a marble pedestal. Inside it was a single large crystal, surrounded by six slight depressions on a red velvet cushion.

The Seventh Crystal was bigger and more beautiful than Chris had dreamed. He took it out of the case and held it gently in his hand. The crystal sparkled with every color of the rainbow.

"Hurry, Chris. It's awake!"

Chris looked down. The dragon was getting

to its feet. Shawn and Jimmy were hemmed up in a corner behind some rocks. The fierce-looking dragon stood up on its hind legs and blew a long stream of blue fire into the air.

Chris stuffed the crystal inside his shirt, drew his sword, and jumped off the rock, landing on the dragon's back. The dragon was furious. It shook, twisted, and turned, trying to throw off the intruder. Chris stabbed at the rocklike scales, but the sword just hit with a clank and bounced off.

The dragon turned its monstrous head and blew more fire. It roared more loudly, swung its mighty tail, and stamped the ground in anger.

Stalactites fell from the cavern ceiling, narrowly missing Shawn and Jimmy. The dragon turned its head again, and this time Chris struck, thrusting the sword deep into the dragon's soft throat. He drove it in all the way to the hilt, and the dragon fell to one knee.

Chris pulled out the sword and stabbed the beast again and again until he could hardly lift his arm. The dragon swayed and then started to fall.

Sweat ran down Chris's face, stinging his eyes, and at last the monster went down.

"Where are you, Chris?" Jimmy shouted.

Chris made a silent wish to be visible again. Jimmy rushed to him. "Are you all right?"

"Tired, but still here. How about you?"

"Great. Did you find it . . . the Seventh Crystal?"

The crystal sparkled in the dim light of the cave as Chris held it out for them to see. Shawn scooped it out of his hand. "So what do we do now? Click our heels together and tell it to take us home?"

"I don't think it works that way." Chris took the crystal back and gingerly put it inside his shirt. "If we want out, we have to finish the game."

CHAPTER 12

"I just hope you're not taking us around in circles again."

"Oh, give it a rest, Shawn." Jimmy glared at him. "Chris is doing the best he can."

Chris stopped. "Somebody's coming."

"Good." Shawn moved to the center of the road. "We'll flag them down and ask for directions to the palace."

"No. Get off the road. Now." Chris grabbed Jimmy's arm and pulled him behind some trees.

Shawn didn't budge. He waited until the riders came thundering around the corner.

There were five of them, towering knights on black horses.

The horses skidded to a stop in a cloud of dust. Three of them circled around behind Shawn. The leader studied him. "Are you the warrior?"

"Me?" Shawn squeaked. "N-No. I'm just a kid."

The leader drew his sword. "Tell us where the warrior is. Mogg will reward you well."

Shawn looked for a place to run. There wasn't one. "I don't know nothin' about a warrior. I was just walking . . ."

The leader raised his sword and swung at Shawn's head. Halfway to its mark the sword clattered harmlessly to the ground—along with the leader's hand.

"What magic is this?" the leader screamed, cradling the bloody stump of his right arm. "Kill him!"

The other knights urged their horses forward. Suddenly saddles turned and bridles were cut. Two horses reared up and dumped their riders hard.

The leader managed to climb back on his

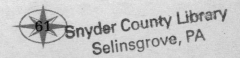

horse, using his one good hand. "This wizard is too powerful for even Mogg to defeat." He sank his spurs into the horse's side and galloped down the road. The knights who were left scrambled to their horses and followed, riding with no saddles and holding on to their horses' manes.

Shawn felt himself being pushed hard. He fell backward. Chris reappeared standing over him, holding the green sword. "The next time I tell you to get off the road—do it."

Chapter 13

"We made it. This has to be the Valley of Zon, and that"— Chris pointed to an ancient structure with tall columns and several stone statues in the front—"has to be the palace."

"Then what are we waiting for?" Shawn asked. "Let's go down and get it over with." He looked at Chris sheepishly. "That is, if you say so."

"I don't think we should charge right up there and go in the front door." Chris rubbed his chin. "The note that came with the game said to take the secret path to the palace."

"I remember that," Jimmy said. "It also told you that the stars would show the way."

Chris fingered the gold necklace the wizard had given him. It didn't feel any different. "Maybe we have to get a little closer to the palace for it to work."

Staying under cover of the trees, the three boys advanced to the palace grounds and hid behind a tall hedge.

"Man, those statues look like real people," Shawn whispered.

"That's because they are, or at least used to be before Mogg got them." Chris held out the necklace. When he faced north, the middle star began to glow.

They followed the hedge until it ended. Chris peeked around it. There was no more cover between them and the palace. Carefully he stepped past the hedge. The ground gave way, and he was falling. He landed flat on his back on a long, slick sheet of metal and started to slide. It was like riding the giant chute at the amusement park. At the end it slowed down and he jumped off. Jimmy and Shawn slid down behind him.

"That was so cool." Jimmy jumped off. "I wouldn't mind trying that again."

"Maybe later." Chris held out the necklace. It didn't glow anymore. "We must be inside the palace."

They went through a heavy iron door and up some stone steps. A second door led to a large hall. At the end was a set of double doors.

Chris pushed the doors open. "This must be the throne room."

Inside, standing gracefully on some steps at the end of a red carpet, was another statue. Chris held his breath. It was the girl in the fountain back home. She was holding out her hands in a pleading gesture.

On either side of the statue were fierce stone lions. One had its mouth open as if snarling at any unwanted visitors.

"What do we do now?" Shawn asked. "I don't see any princess."

"On the contrary," boomed a loud voice that made Chris's ears ring. *"You're looking at her."*

There was a cloud of blue smoke at the front

of the throne room, and in the midst of it a giant appeared. He had two heads and long feathery wings growing from his sides. He put one of the wings around the statue. *"This,"* the giant laughed, *"is the great Princess Darvina."*

Chris tried to turn invisible, but it didn't work.

"Your feeble magic is no match for Mogg. You have failed, warrior. Give me the crystal."

"You mean this crystal?" Chris pulled it out of his shirt. "Heads up!" He tossed it across the room to Shawn.

Both of the giant's faces turned purple with rage. *"Give it to me!"*

Shawn tossed it to Jimmy. "Sorry, your Moggness. I don't have it anymore."

The giant pointed one of his clawlike fingers at Shawn. Instantly the boy turned to stone.

"Separate!" Chris shouted. "Don't let him get the crystal."

Jimmy hid behind one of the lions. "What should I do with it?"

Chris pulled his sword and was about to

charge the giant when he remembered the clue. "The old woman at the beginning of the game. Remember, Jimmy? She told us the only way to save the princess was in the lion's—"

"*Nooooo,*" Mogg thundered. Jimmy watched in stunned horror as Mogg shifted his finger in Chris's direction. Chris was turned to stone in the middle of his attack.

The giant turned to Jimmy. The small boy cowered behind the statue. He reached around the lion and put the crystal in its open mouth for safekeeping.

Mogg's form started to change, as if he were melting, and he screamed in agony. Instead of a giant he was now a two-headed eagle. He spread his wings and flew through an open window, disappearing from sight.

Chris was the first to change back. "What happened?"

Shawn was next. Jimmy explained that Mogg had turned them both to stone and was just about to get the crystal when Jimmy had stuffed it into the lion's mouth.

Chris grinned. "That was the clue I was

about to give you. The old woman said the lion's mouth at the palace was the only way to save the princess. You did it, Jimmy!"

"Yes, Jimmy, you did." A soft voice came from the steps. The statue had turned into a beautiful girl. She walked down the steps and kissed Jimmy lightly on the cheek. Then she moved to Chris, her flawless face inches from his. "I am forever in your debt, warrior. How can I repay you?"

Chris turned red and looked at the floor.

"I can't believe this." Shawn stepped up to the princess. "He wants to get out of this stupid game."

The princess looked puzzled. "Game?"

"Yeah, you know, as in go home, scram, outta here."

"I see." The princess gently took the gold chain with the stars from Chris's neck and placed it around her own. "Is it your wish to go home, warrior?"

Chris nodded shyly.

"Remember this, warrior. The people in the country of Gothan and the Palace of Zon are deeply grateful. We will always be here if you need us." She put both hands on the magic stars and closed her eyes.

Suddenly Chris felt as if he were traveling backward against the wind, spinning faster and faster—until he blacked out.

CHAPTER 14

 Chris's eyes fluttered open. He had on his usual clothes, and he was lying in the grass near the fountain. He sat up and stared. The statue was gone. All that was left was the marble platform where the girl used to be.

Jimmy and Shawn were crawling to their feet.

Shawn looked around. "We're back!" He sat on the edge of the fountain. "That was some wild trip."

"I wonder how long we've been gone?"

Jimmy sat down near Shawn. "My mom is probably going nuts."

Chris looked at his watch in disbelief. He wasn't sure when the adventure had started, but the whole thing hadn't lasted more than a few minutes.

"Where you been, man?" Cliff trotted up the sidewalk. "I've been looking everywhere. Are you ready for me to trash these dudes?" He doubled up his fist and shook it threateningly at Jimmy.

Shawn paused. He looked from Chris to Jimmy, stood up slowly, and put his face close to Cliff's. "Get lost, dweebo."

Cliff's mouth fell open.

"Don't you understand English? I said get lost." Shawn helped Chris to his feet. "Or I'll sic the warrior here on you."

Chris tried to hide a smile.

"You've lost it, Shawn." Cliff spat on the ground and turned to go. "Me and you are through."

"That's fine with me. I'm hanging with a new gang now—the Three Musketeers."

GARY PAULSEN
ADVENTURE GUIDE

MEDIEVAL KNIGHTHOOD

In the Middle Ages, when a boy reached the age of seven he could become a *page* and begin training to become a knight. He would be sent to the castle of a relative to learn about weapons, tend falcons, and run errands. He would also spend part of his time with the lady of the castle, learning courtesy. A page's main training took place in the tiltyard, where he would run, wrestle, and learn to use a blunted sword, wield a lance, and ride a horse.

At the age of fourteen a page became a *squire.* He would then be sent to serve a particular knight. During this time he would work on perfecting his fighting skills, but his main duty was to attend the knight. His duties included helping the knight to dress, carving his meat, and sleeping on the floor beside his bed. The squire accompanied the knight to tournaments, and even to war.

When he reached the age of twenty-one, if the money was available for his initiation and for the necessary equipment, a squire could become a *knight.*

Several squires were usually dubbed knights during one ceremony. The initiation began with a ceremonial bath. Then the young men had their beards and heads shaved. Each candidate was clothed in a white tunic, black hose, and a red cloak.

They were now ready for the *vigil,* in which they would spend the entire night awake, standing or kneeling in a church at the altar steps.

The formal initiation took place the following morning. The candidate's sponsor would fit him in his armor, including his golden spurs and his sword. The new knight would then kneel and receive the *dubbing,* a light tap on each shoulder with the flat part of a swordblade, which proclaimed that he was a true knight and warrior of the realm.

Don't miss all the exciting action!

Read the other action-packed books in Gary Paulsen's WORLD OF ADVENTURE!

The Legend of Red Horse Cavern

Will Little Bear Tucker and his friend Sarah Thompson have heard the eerie Apache legend many times. Will's grandfather especially loves to tell them about Red Horse—an Indian brave who betrayed his people, was beheaded, and now haunts the Sacramento Mountain range, searching for his head. To Will and Sarah it's just a story—until they decide to explore a newfound mountain cave, a cave filled with dangerous treasures.

Deep underground, Will and Sarah uncover an old chest stuffed with a million dollars. But now armed bandits are after them. When they find a gold Apache statue hidden in a skull, it seems Red Horse is hunting them too. Then they lose their way, and each step they take in the damp, dark cavern could be their last.

Rodomonte's Revenge

Friends Brett Wilder and Tom Houston are video game whizzes. So when a new virtual reality arcade called Rodomonte's Revenge opens near their home, they make sure that they are its first customers. The game is awesome. There are flaming fire rivers to jump, beastly buzz-bugs to fight, and ugly tunnel spiders to escape. If they're good enough they'll face

Rodomonte, an evil giant waiting to do battle within his hidden castle.

But soon after they play the game, strange things start happening to Brett and Tom. The computer is taking over their minds. Now everything that happens in the game is happening in real life. A buzz-bug could gnaw off their ears. Rodomonte could smash them to bits. Brett and Tom have no choice but to play Rodomonte's Revenge again. This time they'll be playing for their lives.

Escape from Fire Mountain

". . . please, anybody . . . fire . . . need help."

That's the urgent cry thirteen-year-old Nikki Roberts hears over the CB radio the weekend she's left alone in her family's hunting lodge. The message also says that the sender is trapped near a bend in the river. Nikki knows it's dangerous, but she has to try to help. She paddles her canoe downriver, coming closer to the thick black smoke of the forest fire with each stroke. When she reaches the bend, Nikki climbs onshore. There, covered with soot and huddled on a rock ledge, sit two small children.

Nikki struggles to get the children to safety. Flames roar around them. Trees splinter to the ground. But as Nikki tries to escape the fire, she doesn't know that two poachers are also hot on her trail. They fear that she and the children have seen too much of their illegal operation—and they'll do anything to keep the kids from making it back to the lodge alive.

The Rock Jockeys

Devil's Wall.

Rick Williams and his friends J.D. and Spud—the Rock Jockeys—are attempting to become the first and youngest climbers to ascend the north face of their area's most treacherous mountain. They're also out to discover if a B-17 bomber rumored to have crashed into the mountain years ago is really there.

As the Rock Jockeys explore Devil's Wall, they stumble upon the plane's battered shell. Inside, they find items that seem to have belonged to the crew, including a diary written by the navigator. Spud later falls into a deep hole and finds something even more frightening: a human skull and bones. To find out where they might have come from, the boys read the navigator's story in the diary. It reveals a gruesome secret that heightens the dangers the mountain might hold for the Rock Jockeys.

Hook 'Em, Snotty!

Bobbie Walker loves working on her grandfather's ranch. She hates the fact that her cousin Alex is coming up from Los Angeles to visit and will probably ruin her summer. Alex can barely ride a horse and doesn't know the first thing about roping. There is no way Alex can survive a ride into the flats to round up wild cattle. But Bobbie is going to have to let her tag along anyway.

Out in the flats the weather turns bad. Even worse, Bobbie knows that she'll have to watch out for the

Bledsoe boys, two mischievous brothers who are usually up to no good. When the boys rustle the girls' cattle, Bobbie and Alex team up to teach the Bledsoes a lesson. But with the wild bull Diablo on the loose, the fun and games may soon turn deadly serious.

Danger on Midnight River

Daniel Martin doesn't want to go to Camp Eagle Nest. He wants to spend the summer as he always does: with his uncle Smitty in the Rocky Mountains. Daniel is a slow learner, but most other kids call him retarded. Daniel knows that at camp, things are only going to get worse. His nightmare comes true when he and three bullies must ride the camp van together.

On the trip to camp Daniel is the butt of the bullies' jokes. He ignores them and concentrates on the roads outside. He thinks they may be lost. As the van crosses a wooden bridge, the planks suddenly give way. The van plunges into the raging river below. Daniel struggles to shore, but the driver and the other boys are nowhere to be found. It's freezing, and night is setting in. Daniel faces a difficult decision. He could save himself . . . or risk everything to try to rescue the others too.

The Gorgon Slayer

Eleven-year-old Warren Trumbull has a strange job. He works for Prince Charming's Damsel in Distress

Rescue Agency, saving people from hideous monsters, evil warlocks, and wicked witches. Then one day Warren gets the most dangerous assignment of all: He must exterminate a Gorgon.

Gorgons are horrible creatures. They have green scales, clawed fingers, and snakes for hair. They also have the power to turn people to stone. Warren doesn't want to be a stone statue for the rest of his life. He'll need all his courage and skill—and his secret plan—to become a true Gorgon slayer.

The Gorgon howls as Warren enters the dark basement to do battle. Warren lowers his eyes, raises his sword and shield, and leaps into action. But will his plan work?

Captive!

Roman Sanchez is trying hard to deal with the death of his dad—a SWAT team member gunned down in the line of duty. But Roman's nightmare is just beginning.

When masked gunmen storm into his classroom, Roman and three other boys are taken hostage. They are thrown into the back of a truck and hauled to a run-down mountain cabin, miles from anywhere. They are bound with rope and given no food. With each passing hour the kidnappers' deadly threats become even more real.

Roman knows time is running out. Now he must somehow put his dad's death behind him so that he and the others can launch a last desperate fight for freedom.

Project: A Perfect World

When Jim Stanton's family moves to a small town in New Mexico, everyone but Jim is happy. His dad has a great job as a research scientist at Folsum Laboratories. His mom has a beautiful new house. Folsum Labs even buys a bunch of new toys for his little sister.

But there's something strange about the town. The people all dress and act alike. Everyone's *too* polite. And they're all eerily obedient to the bosses at Folsum Labs.

Though he was warned not to leave town, Jim wanders into the nearby mountains looking for excitement. There he meets Maria, a mountain girl with a shocking secret that involves Folsum Laboratories, a dangerous mind control experiment, and—most frightening of all—Jim's family.

The Treasure of El Patrón

Tag Jones and his friend Cowboy spend their days diving in the azure water surrounding Bermuda. It's not just for fun—Tag knows that somewhere in the coral reef there's a sunken ship full of treasure. His father died in a diving accident looking for the ship, and Tag won't give up until he finds it.

Then the ship's manifest of the Spanish galleon *El Patrón* turns up, and Tag can barely contain his excitement. *El Patrón* sank in 1614, carrying "unknown cargo." Tag knows that *this* is the ship his father was looking for. And he's not the least bit scared off by the rumors that *El Patrón* is cursed. But when two tourists want Tag to retrieve some mysterious sunken parcels for them, Tag and Cowboy may be in dangerous water, way over their heads!

Skydive!

Jesse Rodriguez has a pretty exciting job for a thirteen-year-old, working at a small flight and skydiving school near Seattle. Buck Sellman, the owner of the school, lets Jesse help out around the airport and is teaching him all about skydiving. Jesse can't wait until he's sixteen and old enough to make his first jump.

Then Robin Waterford walks in with her father one day to sign up for lessons, and strange things start to happen. Photographs that Robin takes of the airfield mysteriously disappear from her locker. And Robin and Jesse discover that someone at the airfield is involved in an illegal transportation operation. Jesse and Robin soon find themselves in the middle of real danger and are forced to make their first skydives very unexpectedly—using only one parachute!

Cool sleuths, hot on the case! Look for these upcoming books from Gary Paulsen's hilarious Culpepper Adventures.

Dunc and Amos Go to the Dogs

Anyone who knows Amos knows that in his case, dogs are definitely *not* man's best friend. Even his own dog growls and shows his teeth whenever Amos is around. Amos isn't exactly fond of Scruff either. But when Scruff gets mixed up in a dognapping scheme, Amos and Dunc have to spring him. Join Gary Paulsen's cool sleuths as they go undercover at the city pound.

Amos and the Vampire

Amos's big sister, Amy, is always dating rejects. But this time her boyfriend was rejected by the grave! He's got pale skin, dark hair, mesmerizing eyes, and an annoying tendency to disappear, and he wants to have the Culpeppers over for a late-night Halloween snack. Can Amos and his best friend, Dunc, stop the vampire before he starts to bite? Or will Amy and her man do a little necking she will never forget? Join Dunc and Amos on their creepiest caper yet.